the Quarreling Book

the Quarreling Book

by Charlotte Zolotow

pictures by Arnold Lobel

HarperCollins*Publishers*

For Elizabeth Janeway

It was a rainy gray morning, and Mr. James forgot to kiss
Mrs. James good-bye when he left for the office.

Mrs. James felt quite cross because of this and because the rain made the day so gray. So when Jonathan James came down for breakfast, she was sharp with him.

"Oh, for goodness' sake!" she said. "Why did you wear that shirt again today? It's filthy!"

The shirt looked clean to Jonathan, and he thought her unfair. Because of this and because the rain made the day so gray, he turned on Sally James when she came down for breakfast.

"Can't you ever get down in time?" he said. "You'll be late to school for sure."

The clock said eight-fifteen, which was the time Sally was supposed to come down, and she thought Jonathan was completely unreasonable. Because of this and because the rain made the day so gray, when Sally got to school and met her best friend, Marjorie, in the hall, she looked at her and said, "Where'd you get that awful raincoat? It looks like a boy's."

Marjorie, who thought the raincoat was a beautiful of yellow, felt Sally was very unpleasant, and se of this and because the rain made the day so anyway, when she got home from school and her little brother playing with her dolls she said, do I have to have a little sissy for a brother?"

Eddie, her little brother, always played wi[t]
dolls and she had never minded before, and he th[ought]
her most unkind. Because of this and becau[se]
couldn't go outdoors to play in the rain, Eddie w[ent]
his room and shoved the dog off his bed, where t[he]
was sleeping.

But the dog didn't mind the rain. She thought Eddie was playing so she put her front paws down and her hindquarters up and her tail began wagging.

She pounced on Eddie and they rolled over and wrestling together until the dog won and sat down ddie's chest and began licking his face.

This tickled and made him laugh, and l
laughing so hard that when Marjorie came in look
a pencil for her arithmetic homework, he gave l
best one with a new eraser.

She was so grateful she couldn't help smili
saying, "Thank you very much." She started ou
room and then turned back.

"You really aren't a sissy," she said.

She couldn't find the paper she'd copied the prob-
on, and she had to call up Sally to get them. She
t she was mad at her.

"Hello, Sally?" she said, and she sounded so
lly that Sally was sorry she had said that about the
oat. She gave Marjorie the homework and said,
really not so bad, that raincoat. You just have to
ed to the color." Then she hung up feeling better
an back upstairs, humming to herself.

She met Jonathan at the top of the staircase there, Johnny," she said. "I wasn't late at all." smiled at him so pleasantly that Jonathan said, just teasing you."

"It's O.K.," said Sally.

Just then Mrs. James came into the hall. Jonathan said, "I'll put this in the laundry tonight for sure, Mom." And Mrs. James was so pleased that he remembered she said, "All right, dear. I couldn't have hung the wash in all this rain anyhow. Tomorrow will do as well."

Around five o'clock the sun came out. Everything looked glistening and clean, and the birds began to sing

just as Mr. James came home and gave Mrs. James a grea
warm hello kiss before he went upstairs to wash fo
dinner.